DAISY GETS DRESSED

illustrated by **Clare Beaton**

Barefoot Books
Celebrating Art and Story

Daisy's going to get dressed.

Can you help her look her best?

Where can Daisy's undershirt be?

And how many zigzag things can you see?

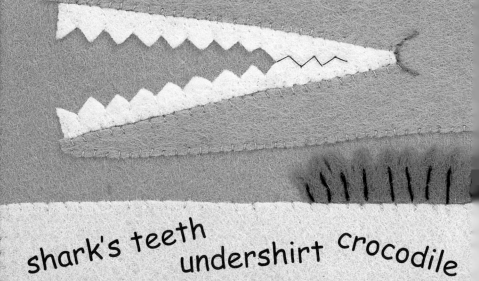

shark's teeth
undershirt crocodile

dinosaur mountains bird lightning tulips grass leaves pine trees
saw

Where can Daisy's T-shirt be?

And how many checkered things can you see?

toy blocks flag checkerboard waffles

tablecloth

fly swatter

buildings

dog's coat

bowl

paint box

tennis racket

T-shirt

Where can Daisy's new tights be?

And how many striped things can you see?

rainbow   bee   house   raccoon

ladder   cat   comb   zebra   candy cane   jug   fish   tights

Where can Daisy's miniskirt be?

And how many wavy things can you see?

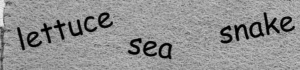
lettuce sea snake octopus

hair   spaghetti   slide   caterpillars   yak   miniskirt   smoke

Where can Daisy's cardigan be?

And how many flowery things can you see?

curtains

teapot

cushion

armchair   mug   garland   seed packets   cardigan

Where can Daisy's
sun hat be?

And how many starry
things can you see?

night sky   barrette   Christmas tree

hooting star   fireworks   sun hat   starfish
fairy wand   sheriff's badge   earring

Where can Daisy's rubber boots be?

And how many spotted things can you see?

cookies
bow
frog
leopard
rubber boots

snow globe   car   ladybugs   toadstool   eggs   butterfly

pencil   dog   dice   owl

Where can Daisy's umbrella be?

And how many spiral things can you see?

shells   chameleon   lollipop

sheep   book   monkeys   snails   roses   hose   umbrella

Where can Daisy's backpack be?

And how many diamond things can you see?

pineapple   ring   fishing net

jack-in-the-box   kite   crown   playing cards   window   backpack

Now Daisy's ready to run and play!

What are the clothes she is wearing today?

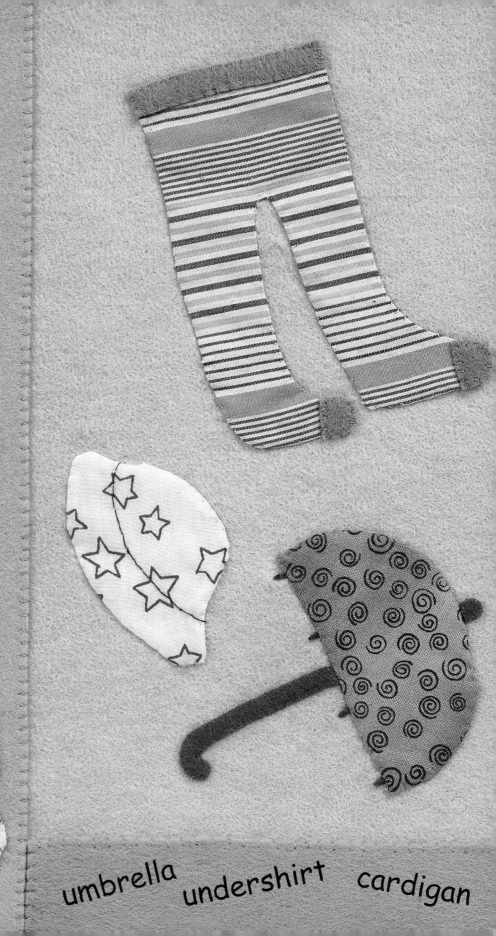

umbrella   undershirt   cardigan

tights   T-shirt   miniskirt   sun hat   backpack   rubber boots

For Richard and Harriet — C. B.

Barefoot Books
2067 Massachusetts Ave
Cambridge, MA 02140

This book was typeset in Cerigo Bold 22 on 28 point and Comic Sans 22 point
The illustrations were prepared in antique fabrics and felt with sequins, buttons,
beads and assorted bric-a-brac

Color transparencies by Jonathan Fisher Photography, Bath
Graphic design by Judy Linard, London. Color separation by Grafiscan, Verona
Printed and bound in Hong Kong by South China Printing
This book has been printed on 100% acid-free paper

Library of Congress Cataloging-in-Publication Data
Beaton, Clare.
    Daisy gets dressed / ; illustrated by Clare Beaton.
        p. cm.
    Summary: A young girl needs help finding different articles of clothing among
the many zigzag, checkered, striped, and other patterned objects in her home.
    ISBN 1-84148-794-5 (alk. paper)
    [1. Clothing and dress--Fiction. 2. Pattern perception--Fiction. 3. Stories in
rhyme.]   I. Beaton, Clare, ill. II. Title.
    PZ8.3.B5735Dai 2005
    [E]--dc22

2004021205

1 3 5 7 9 8 6 4 2

Barefoot Books
Celebrating Art and Story

At Barefoot Books, we celebrate art and story with books that open
the hearts and minds of children from all walks of life, inspiring them to read
deeper, search further, and explore their own creative gifts. Taking our
inspiration from many different cultures, we focus on themes that encourage
independence of spirit, enthusiasm for learning, and acceptance of other
traditions. Thoughtfully prepared by writers, artists, and storytellers from
all over the world, our products combine the best of the present with the best
of the past to educate our children as the caretakers of tomorrow.

www.barefootbooks.com